W9-ARV-362

What Kids Say About
Carole Marsh Mysteries . . .

"I love the real locations! Reading the book always makes me want to go and visit them all on our next family vacation. My Mom says maybe, but I can't wait!"

"One day, I want to be a real kid in one of Ms. Marsh's mystery books. I think it would be fun, and I think I am a real character anyway. I filled out the application and sent it in and am keeping my fingers crossed!"

"History was not my favorite subject till I starting reading Carole Marsh Mysteries. Ms. Marsh really brings history to life. Also, she leaves room for the scary and fun."

"I think Christina is so smart and brave. She is lucky to be in the mystery books because she gets to go to a lot of places. I always wonder just how much of the book is true and what is made up. Trying to figure that out is fun!"

"Grant is cool and funny! He makes me laugh a lot!!"

"I like that there are boys and girls in the story of different ages. Some mysteries I outgrow, but I can always find a favorite character to identify with in these books."

"They are scary, but not too scary. They are funny. I learn a lot. There is always food which makes me hungry. I feel like I am there."

Franklin School
Summit Public Schools

What Parents and Teachers Say About Carole Marsh Mysteries . . .

"I think kids love these books because they have such a wealth of detail. I know I learn a lot reading them! It's an engaging way to look at the history of any place or event. I always say I'm only going to read one chapter to the kids, but that never happens—it's always two or three, at least!"
—Librarian

"Reading the mystery and going on the field trip—Scavenger Hunt in hand—was the most fun our class ever had! It really brought the place and its history to life. They loved the real kids characters and all the humor. I loved seeing them learn that reading is an experience to enjoy!"
—4th grade teacher

"Carole Marsh is really on to something with these unique mysteries. They are so clever; kids want to read them all. The Teacher's Guides are chock full of activities, recipes, and additional fascinating information. My kids thought I was an expert on the subject—and with this tool, I felt like it!"
—3rd grade teacher

"My students loved writing their own Real Kids/Real Places mystery book! Ms. Marsh's reproducible guidelines are a real jewel. They learned about copyright and more & ended up with their own book they were so proud of!"
—Reading/Writing Teacher

"The kids seem very realistic—my children seemed to relate to the characters. Also, it is educational by expanding their knowledge about the famous places in the books."

"They are what children like: mysteries and adventures with children they can relate to."

"Encourages reading for pleasure."

"This series is great. It can be used for reluctant readers, and as a history supplement."

The Mystery at the

Taj Mahal

INDIA

by Carole Marsh

Copyright ©2014 Carole Marsh/Gallopade International
Current Edition ©September 2014
All rights reserved.
Manufactured in Peachtree City, GA
Ebook edition Copyright ©2014

Carole Marsh Mysteries™ and its skull colophon are the property of Carole Marsh and Gallopade International.

Published by Gallopade International/Carole Marsh Books. Printed in the United States of America.

Senior Editor: Janice Baker
Assistant Editor: Gabrielle Humphrey
Cover Design: John Hanson
Content Design and Illustrations: Randolyn Friedlander

Gallopade International is introducing SAT words that kids need to know in each new book we publish. The SAT words are bold in the story. Look for this special logo beside each word in the glossary. Happy Learning!

Gallopade is proud to be a member and supporter of these educational organizations and associations:

American Booksellers Association
American Library Association
International Reading Association
National Association for Gifted Children
The National School Supply and Equipment Association
The National Council for the Social Studies
Museum Store Association
Association of Partners for Public Lands
Association of Booksellers for Children
Association for the Study of African American Life and History
National Alliance of Black School Educators

This book is a complete work of fiction. All events are fictionalized, and although the names of real people are used, their characterization in this book is fiction. All attractions, product names, or other works mentioned in this book are trademarks of their respective owners and the names and images used in this book are strictly for editorial purposes; no commercial claims to their use is claimed by the author or publisher.

Without limiting the rights under copyright reserved above, no part of this publication may be reproduced, stored in or introduced into a retrieval system, or transmitted, in any form or by any means (electronic, mechanical, photocopying, recording or otherwise), without the prior written permission of both the copyright owner and the above publisher of this book.

The scanning, uploading, and distribution of this book via the Internet or via any other means without the permission of the publisher is illegal and punishable by law. Please purchase only authorized electronic editions and do not participate in or encourage electronic piracy of copyrightable materials. Your support of the author's rights is appreciated.

30 Years Ago . . .

As a mother and an author, one of the fondest periods of my life was when I decided to write mystery books for children. At this time (1979), kids were pretty much glued to the TV, something parents and teachers complained about the way they do about web surfing and video games today.

I decided to set each mystery in a real place—a place kids could go and visit for themselves after reading the book. And I also used real children as characters. Usually a couple of my own children served as characters, and I had no trouble recruiting kids from the book's location to also be characters.

Also, I wanted all the kids—boys and girls of all ages—to participate in solving the mystery. And, I wanted kids to learn something as they read—something about the history of the location. And I wanted the stories to be funny. That formula of real+scary+smart+fun served me well.

I love getting letters from teachers and parents who say they read the book with their class or child, then visited the historic site and saw all the places in the mystery for themselves. What's so great about that? What's great is that you and your children have an experience that bonds you together forever—something you shared; something you all cared about at the time; and something that crossed all age levels: a good story, a good scare, and a good laugh!

30 years later,

Carole Marsh

Christina Mimi Papa Grant

"Mystery Girl"

Hey, kids! As you see—here we are ready to embark on another of our exciting Carole Marsh Mystery adventures! You know, in "real life," I keep very close tabs on Christina, Grant, and their friends when we travel. However, in the mystery books, they always seem to slip away from Papa and me so that they can try to solve the mystery on their own!

I hope you will go to www.carolemarshmysteries.com and apply to be a character in a future mystery book! Well, the *Mystery Girl* is all tuned up and ready for "take-off!"

Gotta go...Papa says so! Wonder what I've forgotten this time?

Happy "Armchair Travel" Reading,

Mimi

About the Characters

Christina: Mysterious things really do happen to her! Hobbies: soccer, Girl Scouts, anything crafty, hanging out with Mimi, and going on new adventures

Grant: Always manages to fall off boats, back into cactuses, and find strange clues—even in real life! Hobbies: camping, baseball, computer games, math, and hanging out with Papa

Mimi is Carole Marsh, children's book author and creator of Carole Marsh Mysteries, Around the World in 80 Mysteries, Three Amigos Mysteries, Baby's First Mysteries, and many others.

Papa is Bob Longmeyer, the author's real-life husband, who really does wear a tuxedo, cowboy boots and hat, fly an airplane, captain a boat, speak in a booming voice, and laugh a lot!

Travel around the world with Christina and Grant as they visit famous places in 80 countries, and experience the mysterious happenings that always seem to follow them!

Books in This Series

Table of Contents

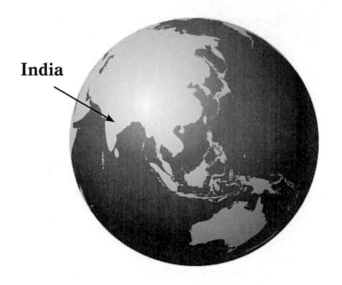

India

AGRA

INDIA

1

a floating surprise

The wind tossed sheets of sand across the hot Indian desert. Despite the storm, Christina's camel trudged on, bobbing and swaying beneath her.

"Don't get lost, Little One," she whispered into her camel's ear, before diving under her cloak.

The sandstorm stopped and there was silence. Christina tugged the cloak away from her face and peered up at the darkening sky. In the distance, a sparkling domed structure carved from sand slowly rose up from the earth.

The wind picked up again, taking her camel's footprints with it. Rain fell, then clumps of snow, changing the hills of sand into glistening frosty mountains.

Christina woke up shivering. She tucked her thin blue airline blanket up under her chin, images of camels and snowy deserts still swirling in her head.

Except for the humming of the engines, the cabin was quiet. It was late. A few passengers were still awake, either reading or working on their laptops. The others, including her little brother Grant and her grandparents Mimi and Papa, were sound asleep in their seats.

Christina stretched to turn on her overhead light.

PLUNK!

The in-flight magazine she was reading before she dozed off flopped to the floor. Smiling up at her from the glossy pages was a young Indian family wearing colorful robes in front of the Taj Mahal.

She leaned down to pick up the magazine.

BONK!

"I'm so sorry!" she cried.

"No, it's really all right!" said a man with a British accent. He wore a blue pinstripe suit and sunflower-yellow tie. He smiled at her from across the aisle. A flight attendant in a red uniform, with her hair pulled back in a perfect bun, passed out extra blankets nearby.

"Are you all right?" asked the man. He pushed his gold-rimmed glasses back onto his nose and handed Christina the magazine.

"I'm fine," she said. "Mr. Hawke, I never thanked you for switching seats with my grandfather. He was a little cramped there."

"Not a problem," he insisted, holding up his hand. "Your grandmother said she's a mystery writer. It must be exciting getting to travel with your grandparents all over the world."

"Yes, sir," said Christina. "And if you can believe it, my brother and I usually get caught up in a mystery of our own on these trips! Once, we solved the clues and found an ancient treasure in—" Christina was cut off.

"Extra blanket?" the flight attendant asked.

"Yes, thank you," said Christina.

"I want pizza and ice cream, please!" mumbled Grant.

Christina turned to her little brother. "Grant, you awake?" His face was plastered to the shuttered window. Drool seeped from the side of his mouth.

"I guess not," she said softly.

Christina heard the soft click of a seatbelt, and noticed Mr. Hawke head down the aisle and reappear on the other side of the cabin. A tall man wearing a dark-colored turban and a beige suit stood up to shake his hand. Words from their conversation, like "package" and "delivery," floated over to Christina.

"SSHHHH!" The flight attendant put a finger to her lips to quiet the men and led them to behind a curtain.

Christina flipped to the map of India in the back of her in-flight magazine. With her finger, she traced the route from her home on the east coast of the U.S., all the way across the Atlantic Ocean to India, a huge country in southern Asia. It looked to Christina like India's neighbors— Pakistan, Afghanistan, Nepal, and China—had to hold onto the country to keep it from slipping into the Indian Ocean.

Christina unbuckled her seatbelt and stood up to stretch. Mimi and Papa were sound asleep on the other side of the cabin. Mimi snuggled in her favorite red airplane slippers and red facemask, while Papa stretched his long legs out comfortably in front of him. His white Stetson hat rested on his chest.

Christina sat back down and checked her cell phone. She breathed a sigh of relief. "Just two more hours," she murmured. Her long brown hair popped with static electricity. She pulled it back with a clip and adjusted her seat to get some rest.

"Hey, Christina, let me out," whined Grant, elbowing his sister. "Christina, wake up!"

Christina opened one eye. "I wasn't asleep, Grant. What do you want?"

Grant stood up. His curly blonde hair was matted down on the right side, making his head look lopsided.

"I have to go to the bathroom," he said, half-asleep.

Christina pulled her legs up so her brother could pass. "Don't get lost, OK?"

"Ha ha, very funny," he mumbled. After a few minutes, Grant returned with a confused look on his face. "Which way is the bathroom again?"

With her eyes still closed, she said, "Just go straight up this aisle. It'll be on your left."

Grant trudged off. Ten minutes later, he tapped his sister on the shoulder. "Hey, let me back in."

"Your shirt! It's soaking wet," she whispered. "What happened?"

"I was trying to wash my hands without sinking this paper boat." Grant held up a miniature boat folded out of paper.

"Why did you take a paper boat into the bathroom?" she asked, bewildered.

Grant's hair was still lopsided. Christina stifled a laugh. "I didn't!" he answered. "It was floating in the sink when I got in there."

"Is that what took you so long? You were playing with this boat?" she asked.

"No," replied Grant. "I was about to go in, but a lady cut in front of me," he explained. "She said nature was calling her, but I never saw a phone in the bathroom!"

2

deli or
delhi bound?

Christina checked her phone and yawned. "It's almost midnight," she said. "I wish I could sleep!"

"Midnight?" asked Grant, rubbing his head. "There's no way the sandwich shop will be open this late," he whined.

"Sandwich shop?" asked Christina.

"Yeah! Papa said we're flying to a deli in Indiana," explained Grant.

Christina's mouth fell open. "All this time you thought we were going to a deli in Indiana?"

Grant nodded.

Christina smiled. "Grant, we're going to Delhi, India."

Grant cocked his head to the side. "India? But, that's on a whole new continent! That deli must have really good sandwiches for Papa to travel to another continent to get them!"

Christina shook her head. "Delhi is a city in India. See?" She showed Grant the map. "New Delhi is the capital, and it's actually located in Delhi."

"We crossed the Atlantic Ocean?" he asked. "No wonder I'm so hungry!"

Christina scanned the cabin. "I'll see if I can find someone," she whispered. "Stay here, OK?"

Grant nodded.

Christina was almost to the curtained area when she turned to look back at her little brother. A woman with long, wavy, dark hair and flowing robes walked toward her. She paused and hovered next to Grant but kept her eyes facing forward.

Just then, a man stood up and blocked Christina's view of her brother. She had to duck under his arm to get back to her seat. But by then, the woman was gone!

Deli or Delhi Bound?

"Who was that?" she asked Grant. The faint scent of lavender hung in the air. "What did she want?"

Grant shrugged. "Who was who? I didn't see anybody. Did you get me a snack?" he asked hopefully.

Christina's heart skipped a beat. "Come with me," she ordered. "We'll find a snack together."

The kids poked their head through the thick blue curtain. "Hello-ooo," called Christina.

"Hello-ooo," echoed Grant.

"Anyone back here?" asked Christina.

"Anyone back here?" repeated Grant.

Christina glared at her brother. "Stop copying me!"

"Stop copying me," he repeated and smiled coyly.

Christina couldn't help but smile back. She pulled the curtain aside.

It was *too* quiet behind the curtain. A coffee maker, microwave oven, and sink took up one counter, while shiny cabinets lined the opposite side.

Without warning, the plane bumped and shifted. The movement tossed Christina and Grant against the counter and onto the floor.

PLUNK!

A cabinet door popped open and a black leather bag slid out. The initials "MM" were embroidered in gold above the zipper. The bag gaped open as Christina lurched over to it. Inside, she saw long objects covered in sparkling jewels. They were individually wrapped in plastic bags.

"We're going to crash!" moaned Grant, rubbing his aching knee.

Christina helped him up off the floor. "No, we're not," she whispered. "It was just a little turbulence, that's all."

Grant pleaded with his sister. "Turbo or not, I want to go back to my seat!"

"We can't leave this bag out," she said.

Grant gasped. "What are those sparkly things?" he asked, bending down to touch them.

Christina stopped him. "We'd better not! Someone might see us! Well, here goes." She lifted the heavy bag by its handles. Its contents clinked when she shoved the bag back into the cabinet. She closed the door and turned to go.

WHOOSH! Christina and Grant jumped as a manicured hand suddenly slid the curtain back. The flight attendant with the bun entered. Christina spied the name "Matilta" on her nametag.

"What are you kids doing back here?" she hissed. Her dark eyes darted to the cabinet, which had popped open again. "You need to go back to your seats now!"

Christina stuttered, "I...I...I–"

The woman pointed her finger toward the aisle. "Now!"

Grant whispered, "Does this mean I don't get a snack?"

3

crossing time zones

DING!

The captain's smooth voice floated over the loudspeaker. "We'll be arriving at Indira Gandhi International Airport thirty minutes ahead of schedule." Passengers stirred from their long naps, stretching their arms in the air and twisting their stiff torsos.

"Is it really midnight?" asked Grant, peeking over his sister's shoulder through the window.

"Uh huh," she mumbled. "A little after."

Grant's blue eyes shone bright. "I never get to stay up this late!"

"We should sleep when we get to the hotel," she said. "That way, we won't have jet lag tomorrow."

"What's jet lag?" asked Grant.

"It happens when you travel across time zones. You get off your normal sleep schedule, so you have to trick your body into thinking it's one time when it's really another."

"Your mind is attached to your body, isn't it?" he asked.

Christina sighed. "It is."

"Then how can you trick it?" he asked.

"Think about this," she suggested. "It's 2:30 in the afternoon at home—"

"And it's midnight here?" he interrupted.

"Right," she said. "Your body still thinks it's 2:30, so that's why we have to trick it or you won't be able to sleep. If you don't sleep, you'll get jet lag tomorrow and feel really sleepy and be really grumpy."

Grant looked at his arms and legs and tried to understand how they could still think it was only 2:30 in the afternoon.

Crossing Time Zones

The plane bumped and jolted as it landed. A line of smiling flight attendants met passengers disembarking the airplane. "Welcome to Indira International Airport! Have a pleasant stay in India!"

Christina leaned down and whispered into Grant's ear, "That mean flight attendant isn't here!"

4

oh, fearless one!

Terminal Three of Indira Gandhi International Airport bustled with travelers.

"Who are you waving to?" asked Christina.

"Those giant hands!" cried Grant. He pointed to a wall above a sign that read "Customs and Immigration." Nine giant metallic hands surrounded by hundreds of shiny bronze discs jutted from the wall.

"See? They're waving to us!" he exclaimed, trying to imitate the hand gestures.

"I read about those on the plane!" said Christina excitedly. "They're called *mudras*, or hand gestures. Each of the hand gestures means something different."

"My favorite is that one," decided Mimi, pointing to a massive shiny hand with an open palm and slightly bent fingers.

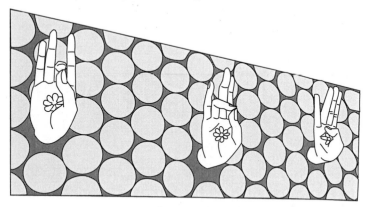

"That was my favorite, too," said Christina. "I wrote down what it's called. In the Hindi language, it's known as the *abhaya mudra,* or 'fearless gesture.'"

"I'm fearless!" announced Grant. He moved his hands to imitate the gesture and stomped around.

"Hey, Oh, Fearless One," said Papa, "get back in line. Here's your passport. They're ready for us!"

Oh, Fearless One!

Outside the air-conditioned airport, a searing blast of hot air hit the family. "Wow! I never expect it to be so hot at night," exclaimed Mimi.

Papa removed his Stetson hat and fanned his face. "Phewee! It's hotter than a chili pepper in a Texas desert out here!"

"Well, if twenty-two million Delhiites can get used to it, then so can we," declared Mimi.

To get downtown, they decided to take a private taxi with a 'Radio Taxi' sign on the car.

"Welcome to Delhi, India, the City of Cities!" a dark-skinned man with jet-black hair announced. "Where are you headed?" he asked in a rolling British accent.

"To the Imperial Hotel, please," said Papa.

"Very good choice!" the taxi driver said and helped Papa load their bags into the trunk. "My name is Sunil. Please," he said, motioning to Papa to get in the front seat of the cab.

"Hang on!" Sunil warned. He quickly pulled into the bustling traffic. Even though it was way past midnight in Delhi, the city was alive!

"AAAAHHH!" hollered Grant, scrunching up into a ball. "Papa, why are *you* driving? You're on the wrong side of the road! I take it back! I am *not* the Fearless One after all!" he wailed.

Sunil smiled and waved into the rearview mirror. "Yoo-hoo, children! I'm right here. I'm driving the car, I promise!"

"Huh?" said Grant. He straightened up. "But why are you sitting in the passenger's seat and driving on the wrong side of the road?"

"In India, as in England, we drive on the left side of the road," he explained. He honked when a cycle rickshaw crossed in front of him. "And I sit on the right side of the car. See my steering wheel?"

"Uh, huh," said Grant. "Wow, so everything is opposite! Wait till I tell my friends back home!"

Mimi smiled. "Is it far to the hotel?"

"If we're lucky, it will only take about twenty minutes to get there," Sunil replied.

Papa spoke up. "Sunil, earlier you called Delhi the 'City of Cities.' Why did you call it that?"

Sunil honked his horn again to warn **pedestrians** crossing the road to get out of the way. "Delhi is called that because throughout its long history, it has been occupied many times by different world powers. In fact, it's been continuously inhabited since the sixth century, serving as the capital of many kingdoms and empires," he explained.

"We learned about the East India Company in school," said Christina. "It was an English trading company. Didn't it control India in the 1800s?"

"Yes, they defeated the Maratha Empire in 1803 and controlled much of the trade in India," said Sunil. He looked over his shoulder and changed lanes. "They traded things like silk, tea, and spices. After the war, however, the British Raj, or Empire, took over."

"You said there were other empires too?" asked Grant. "What happened to them?"

"Before the British Raj, the Mughal and Maratha Empires controlled India," he explained. "You must find time to visit the Taj Mahal. It is an exquisite example of architecture of the Mughal Emperor Shah Jahan. He controlled a good deal of India around 350 years ago."

Christina smiled. "We do plan to visit the Taj Mahal! I really want to see it!"

"Me too!" exclaimed Grant.

Sunil smiled back at the kids in the rearview mirror. "It is so good to see such enthusiasm in young people."

Mimi asked, "Sunil, do you happen to know the name of a personal driver? We'd like to visit a few places while we're here in India."

"I have another, much bigger car just for that purpose," he announced, passing Papa his business card. "I hope you will call me to arrange a time."

Sunil continued down a cobblestone drive lined with swaying palm trees and flanked by manicured green lawns. He stopped in front of the Imperial Hotel.

5

a floating clue

Christina felt like a princess in a palace when she stepped into the sparkling Imperial Hotel lobby with its gleaming marble floors, bubbling fountains, and magnificent paintings adorning nearly every wall.

Their suite was even more spectacular. Mimi gasped as they entered.

"It's absolutely stunning!" she gushed. She pushed open the tall bi-fold doors leading into the atrium, the second room of their suite. A sparkling chandelier hung from its two-story ceiling.

"We want to get a good night's sleep, so we don't have jet lag tomorrow," warned Papa.

"Oooh, oooh, I know what jet lag is!" said Grant, raising his hand. "It's when you go to another country and the time is different, so you have to be tricky so your body can catch up to it!" Grant cocked his head to the side. "Right?"

"Hmmm," said Papa, rubbing his chin. "That's a great way to put it!"

"Christina taught me!" beamed Grant.

As Christina finished brushing her teeth before bed, she noticed Grant's boat floating in a bowl of water in the bathroom. "Won't your boat get soggy and tear?" she asked.

Grant quickly plucked his boat out of the water. "Oh, yeah!" he gasped. "Hey, there's some writing on the bottom of it." The water had revealed some blurry words written in blue ink.

"Well, aren't you going to read it?" asked Christina.

"But it'll tear if I open it!" he whined.

"I'll make you a new one," she said, grabbing a pad of hotel stationery. She folded it into a paper boat for her brother. "Trade you," she said with a smile.

A Floating Clue

Christina took a deep breath and unfolded the soggy boat. *Could this be a clue?*

She carefully unfolded the paper and saw a scrawled message:

> a moveable cart
> through hollow halls
> a map to explore!

Christina gasped. "Grant, it's a clue!"

The Mystery at the Taj Mahal

6
disappearing act

The next morning, sun filtered through the curtained windows, promising a hot day. The kids woke up to a traditional Indian breakfast in their private dining room.

Among the delicacies rolled in on a cart were sweet *lassi*, a delicious Indian yogurt drink, *paneer paratha*, a cottage cheese-filled wheat bread, and *poori*, a deep fried whole wheat Indian bread with fruit on the side.

Grant slurped his drink. "This *lassi* is sweet!" he said, scrunching his face up. "But it's delicious!"

Christina remembered the "moveable cart" part of the clue. "I'll clean up," she offered after everyone had finished eating.

She searched between plates, inside sugar bowls, and even under the tablecloth that covered the cart. "I give up," she murmured, propping the door open with Mimi's carry-on bag and rolling the cart into the hallway.

Immediately, Christina noticed a woman wearing long, colorful robes standing at one end of the hall. Her long hair seemed to float all around her. "It's the woman from the plane," whispered Christina. "Wait!" she called.

But the woman didn't wait. Instead, she turned a corner and disappeared.

Christina raced down the hallway lined with elegant paintings from another era. She turned the corner, expecting to see the woman, but she was gone.

Instead, Christina found a nook, a dead end with a small ornately-carved teak bench and table. Beside a lamp with an elephant base sat a bottle adorned with colorful jewels.

Christina perched on the edge of the bench and looked around. There was no elevator, no stairwell, and no way for the woman to get away.

Disappearing Act

"There you are!" said Grant, plopping down next to her.

"AAHHH!" Christina jumped. "Don't scare me like that!"

"Sorry!" he said. "But, Mimi wanted me to find you. You left the door open."

"I saw that lady again, the one from the plane," she said.

"The mean one?" asked Grant, making a scowling face.

"No, not her," replied Christina. "The one you said you never saw."

"Oh, yeah!" he said. "You looked like you'd seen a ghost. WHOOOOO!" He wiggled his arms all around, pretending to be a ghost.

"Be serious!" chided Christina.

"Did you talk to her this time?" he asked. "What did she want?"

"*No* to the first question, and *I don't know* to the second," she said crossing her arms. "She disappeared again!"

"You think she might be a ghost?" he asked. "Ghosts appear and disappear, don't they?"

Christina shrugged. "I guess so. Can ghosts leave things behind?"

"Like what?" he asked.

"This bottle?" she asked.

Grant's mouth dropped open. "Oooh! Sparkly!"

Christina plucked the glass top off the bottle. She turned it over and a piece of rolled-up paper slid out. The paper looked old and fragile.

"It's a map," said Grant, touching the old paper. The ink crumbled under his touch.

"It's crumbling. We shouldn't touch it!" warned his sister. The color of the ink used on the map was a color they'd never seen before. It looked like a mixture of purple and gold. "Well," she continued, "this map clue definitely fits in with the paper boat clue: A moveable cart—check! Through hollow halls—check! A map to explore—check!"

"And the map begins at the entrance to this hotel!" exclaimed Grant.

7

chee! chee! chee!

Back in their hotel room, Mimi announced, "I was hoping to do some up close and personal research for my book."

"And what better way to do that than to take a walk in the city," said Papa.

"Can we lead the way?" asked Grant.

"We're right behind you!" answered Papa.

Outside the gates of the Imperial Hotel grounds, Delhi was a completely different place. The further away the family walked, the more crowded it was, the dustier the streets got, and the heavier the traffic became. Cars and buses honked non-stop. Bicycles weaved through traffic, ringing their bells. Women in traditional

Indian *saris* sold colorful cloth out of makeshift stalls by the side of the road.

With Mimi and Papa ambling slowly behind and taking in the sites, Grant and Christina looked at the map.

Christina whispered, "The map takes us north up this street, then west across the street, and finally, south."

Grant and Christina slowed down. "Is that a cow in the road?" asked Grant, pointing and straining his eyes to see. Mimi and Papa caught up to the kids.

"It sure is!" answered Papa.

"Oooh, there's another one!" cried Christina.

Grant pointed. "And another one!" he exclaimed, laughing. "That one has a big bumpy shoulder!"

"It's like no one cares if cows are walking around in the middle of traffic," marveled Christina.

Chee! Chee! Chee!

"Animals, especially cows, are sacred here in India," noted Mimi. She sniffed the air. "Do you smell that?"

"Watch out, Grant!" screeched Christina. "You almost stepped in cow dung!"

Grant sidestepped a giant cow dropping. "Phew! That was a close one!"

Mimi and Papa moved closer to the kids. "I do believe a monkey is trailing us," said Papa.

Grant peeked over his shoulder. "You're right, Papa!"

"What do we do?" asked Christina. "You think it's wild?"

They all looked back at the gray-brown monkey mirroring their every step. "He sure doesn't look house-trained," replied Papa.

"Chee chee chee!" said the monkey.

"Awww!" said Christina, turning around. "It talked to us!"

The monkey bared its teeth.

Christina screeched. "Yikes! What do we do now?"

"Walk faster!" cried Grant.

"Chee chee chee!" repeated the monkey. Its tail flicked back and forth as it chased them along the sidewalk.

Christina stopped and stomped her foot at the monkey. It stopped chasing them and sat down.

"Grant, you have food with you, don't you?" she said accusingly.

"Who? Me? Not me!" he said, waving his hands in front of him.

"Gra-ant!" she said. "Hand it over! He can probably smell it!"

Grant groaned. He reached into his backpack and reluctantly gave up his breakfast bread. "I was saving it for later!" he whined. "There's never food when I'm hungry!"

Christina threw the bread to the monkey. Immediately, three other simians fell from the canopy of trees above them, screeching and feasting on Grant's bread.

"My bread!" groaned Grant.

"Sorry about that!" said Papa. "I don't think our monkey friend would have given up without a fight!"

"I guess not," he said, pouting.

8

another place and time

Christina peeked at the map until they reached a high, red metal gate.

Papa paid to enter what looked to be a park. Once inside the gates, they felt like they'd been transported to another place and time.

"This place is an oasis, smack dab in the middle of a sprawling city!" noted Papa.

Palm trees dotted the beautifully landscaped lawn, where visitors sat, ate, and chatted.

"What is this place?" asked Grant. "It looks like an old city!"

Papa looked at the brochure. "It's called the Jantar Mantar," he replied. "It was used long ago to study the stars and planets."

Jutting up from the lawn were giant structures, reddish-orange in color and peculiarly shaped.

Mimi and Papa sauntered over to a triangular structure.

"Race you!" shouted Grant to his sister.

The two ended up in front of two nearly identical, round three-tiered structures with arches all the way around.

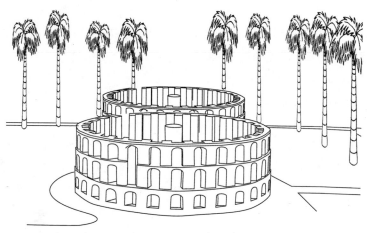

"These are the Ram Yantras," said Christina, reading from a sign. "It says they were used hundreds of years ago to measure the **altitude** of the stars."

"Look, no roof!" cried Grant, peering through an arched window. "It's like a giant wagon wheel with concrete spokes inside!"

Christina followed her brother through the high arched window and onto one of the raised concrete beams. The sun shone through the arches and cast unique shadows.

Grant hopped from beam to beam. He lost his balance and fell to the ground. A poof of dust sprang up to Christina.

"Grant! Are you OK?" she asked. In one swift motion, she slid to the floor.

He coughed. "I'm OK!"

"More arches!" noted Christina. "They hold up the beams."

Grant got up and stretched. "Hey!" he called to two kids. A girl and a boy about the same ages as Christina and Grant were spying on them from a few beams over. Grant hunched down and saw them through the arches. "I see you!" he called.

They leaned down and smiled at Grant and Christina. "You can't catch us!" they teased. They took off running and weaving through the lower arches.

Christina whispered, "Let's go in the opposite direction."

Grant saluted his sister. "Great battle maneuver—cut off the enemy. I like it!"

The two bobbed and weaved through the lower arches until they heard approaching laughter.

Grant jumped out in front of the kids and yelled, "Boo!"

They screamed and then laughed hysterically.

"That was brilliant!" exclaimed the little boy in a British accent.

The four crawled onto one of the beams, still smiling.

"Hi!" said the girl, also with a crisp British accent. "I'm Mahal. This is my brother." The girl had Indian features and bright green eyes.

She giggled and nudged the boy, who looked just like his sister but was a whole foot shorter.

"I'm Taj," said the boy.

Christina smiled back at the kids. "Hi! I'm Christina. This is my younger brother, Grant. Umm, your names, Taj and Mahal..."

Mahal spoke up. "Our mum is from India and our dad is from England. We spend a lot of time between the two countries," she explained.

"Our parents met at the Taj Mahal," said Taj. "So, they decided to name us after the famous monument."

"Have you been to the Taj Mahal yet?" asked Mahal.

"No, we just flew in from the States yesterday," answered Christina. "But, we plan to go there soon."

"I have a confession to make," admitted Mahal. "We saw you back at the hotel. Our dad owns a trading company back in England. And, while he does business here, we stay at the Imperial Hotel. Our mum is visiting family in Mumbai now."

Taj added, "You see, not many people travel with children in India, so we were thrilled to see kids our own ages."

"Mimi—that's our grandmother—is here on business, too," admitted Grant. "She writes children's mysteries. That's why we're here—so she can do research for her next book."

"And," said Christina, clearing her throat, "we may be in the middle of a mystery of our own!"

9

the ram yantra

"When you say mystery..." began Mahal.

"Do you mean the fingerprints and clues kind of mystery?" finished Taj.

"Yep!" said Grant.

"And you say this lady in robes left a bottle clue for you to find?" asked Mahal.

"Yes, I think so—I'm just not sure!" admitted Christina. "She disappeared before I could catch up to her!"

"I haven't seen anyone in the hotel wearing robes like the ones you've described. She may just be passing through," guessed Mahal.

"Just passing through!" laughed Grant. "Get it? Passing through walls?" he said, holding his stomach and laughing out loud.

"Ha ha! Very funny!" said Christina. She wasn't really laughing. In fact, the thought of a ghost leaving clues for her made the hair on the back of her neck stand up.

"Show them the first clue, Christina," urged Grant, still teary-eyed from laughing so hard.

Christina pulled the boat clue out of her backpack and showed it to them. "This used to be a paper boat when Grant found it on the plane. It was floating in the bathroom sink."

"That means someone on the plane left the clue," said Mahal.

"That's right," said Christina. "Well, this clue led to the bottle clue with the map."

"What did the map say you were supposed to do here?" asked Mahal.

Christina shrugged her shoulders. "I'm not sure," she admitted. "The map just led us to this place."

"This place looks really old!" said Grant.

"It is!" said Mahal. "It's over 400 years old. Each of these structures had a different astronomical purpose."

Christina sat down on one of the beams. Mahal sat next to her, and the boys sat across from them. Christina pulled the sparkly bottle from her backpack.

When she saw the bottle, Mahal gasped and covered her mouth with her hands. "Our dad exports bottles just like that," she exclaimed.

Christina remembered the black leather bag with sparkly objects in the airplane.

"Your last name isn't Hawke, is it?" asked Christina.

Taj and Mahal looked at each other and then back at Christina.

"Yes!" they exclaimed in unison.

"But, how did you know?" asked Mahal.

Christina explained. "We met your dad on the plane! He was very kind to our grandparents."

"What a small world!" said Taj.

Christina wondered if there was a connection between their dad and the bottle in her hand.

She pulled the map out of the bottle and unrolled the paper. Just then, the sun shone through the arches of the wall and onto the map Christina was holding. "Did you see that?" she asked. "When I hold the paper in the sun, the map disappears!"

"Yes! And look! A new image appears!" gasped Grant.

"Fascinating!" exclaimed Mahal. "It changes to a bird's eye view of this structure, the Ram Yantra!"

Christina's eyes grew wide. "You're right!" She moved the map in and out of the sun. The map disappeared and then reappeared.

"I see tiny crowns on the map—here, here, and here!" said Grant. "Maybe we're supposed to find those places."

A warm breeze blew in. Christina looked at the map and then around at the raised beams. "Grant, stand over there. OK, stop!"

"Taj, you stand over there," said Mahal, pointing to a spot about twenty feet from where Grant was standing. "OK, stop!"

"The third spot is where we're standing, Mahal," said Christina.

Mahal's eyes widened. She looked down at her feet as though she were standing on a landmine. "Now what?" she squealed.

"Clues come in ones, never twos or threes, at a time!" explained Christina.

"Then, we need to find the center of our human triangle," suggested Grant.

"This is so exciting!" cried Mahal.

Christina smiled at her and nodded. "It really is! Well, here goes!" She looked at her brother and at their new friends and estimated the center point. Christina hopped down off the beam and crawled under the arch. "Come look!" she cried.

Christina heard the pounding of feet above her. "There's a tiny door under this arch!" she exclaimed. She reached up and slid it open. Inside the nook, she felt something smooth and silky. She pulled it out.

"A pouch?" said Grant. He sounded disappointed.

"What were you hoping for?" asked Christina.

"Treasure!" he answered.

Christina opened the golden clasp and poured the contents of the silky, cream-colored pouch into her hand.

"Pearls!" she gasped.

"Treasure!" cried Grant.

10

cannon ball!

Taj and Mahal walked back to the Imperial Hotel with Mimi, Papa, Christina, and Grant. They gawked at cows eating food off the sidewalk, hurried past monkeys hovering in the trees, and rushed past bicycles and honking cars stuck in afternoon traffic.

Back at the hotel, they changed into their swimsuits and crowded under the giant blue umbrellas by the pool to eat fresh fruit and sandwiches. The clear, cool pool looked inviting.

"Christina and Grant mentioned you're planning to visit the Taj Mahal on your trip," said Mahal to Mimi.

Mimi nodded her head. "We are," she answered with a twinkle in her eye. "We'll be traveling in a giant triangle! From here, we'll go south, then east to the Taj Mahal, and then back to Delhi.

"You know, Mahal," Mimi continued, "I've wanted to visit the Taj Mahal ever since I was a little girl." She sighed and looked over at Grant and Christina. "And it's made even more special that we get to share the experience with our grandchildren."

Just then, Taj and Mahal's dad came down to the pool. With a look of surprise on his face, he said, "Wow, what a small world it is indeed." To Mimi and Papa he said, "It's very nice to see you again!"

"Dad!" cried Taj. "These are our new friends, Christina and Grant."

"Yes, I met your friends on the airplane!" he said cheerfully. "Hello! I'm so happy you found Taj and Mahal!"

Christina smiled. "Actually, Taj and Mahal found us!"

Christina watched Taj and Mahal's dad. Nothing about him looked suspicious, but Christina knew from other mysteries they'd solved in the past that even the most innocent-looking people could be up to no good.

She looked around for Grant. For a brief second, she thought they'd left him back at the Jantar Mantar. *That's silly,* she thought. *He was just here!*

"Huh? Grant!" she exclaimed.

Grant was about fifty feet away. He raced toward them, shouting, "Cannon ball!" just before making a leaping jump into the pool. He landed in a perfect ball with a giant SPLASH! A plume of water splattered everyone sitting nearby. He surfaced with a giant smile on his face.

Christina was secretly relieved. She didn't want to have to explain to the adults how they had found the pearls. She didn't want to think about how the bottle holding the map was the very same kind that Mr. Hawke exported out of India.

11

welcome to

neemrana

The next morning, Taj and Mahal unexpectedly showed up in the hotel lobby.

"Thanks for coming to see us off!" said Christina. "I didn't think we'd have a chance to say goodbye before we left!"

"Actually..." said Mahal, lifting her small travel bag up for Christina to see.

Mimi smiled brightly. "Your friends are coming with us!"

"It's OK with your dad?" asked Christina.

Taj and Mahal nodded.

Grant and Taj gave each other a high-five, while Christina and Mahal squealed and jumped up and down.

Their driver, Sunil, pulled up to the hotel in his extra-roomy SUV.

"Wow!" exclaimed Mimi. "You weren't kidding when you said you had a bigger car!"

"I am confident you will find it comfortable," he reported with a smile.

"Oooh, yes!" cried Grant, hopping into the air-conditioned car.

"Next stop: Neemrana Fort-Palace in Neemrana, Rajasthan," announced Sunil.

As they made their way through tangled Delhi traffic, Mimi said, "What this city lacks in order, it more than makes up in colors, sounds, and smells! I have to ask, Sunil, how does anything get done?"

Sunil laughed. "I like to explain it like this," he said over his shoulder. "At university, I studied chemistry. All around us are gazillions and gazillions of different atoms flying around, bumping into each other. But, out of the chaos, comes order. India is much the same way. On the surface, my country might look chaotic, but there is a natural order that comes out of it."

"Well put!" exclaimed Mimi.

Sunil headed southwest from the capital to the state of Rajasthan. They passed through small villages, large cities, and miles and miles of farmland along the way.

Two and a half hours later, Sunil pointed out the window. "Welcome to Neemrana!" he shouted over the bustling sounds of the historical town.

Around a bend and nestled in the hillside was a sprawling fort-palace with archways and terraces.

"The Neemrana Fort-Palace was built in 1467," explained Sunil. "It was converted to a resort in 1986. But don't be fooled! It is like no hotel you've ever been to. And beware! There are plenty of nooks and crannies and passageways to get lost in!"

Sunil parked at the curb in front of the Neemrana Fort-Palace and helped everyone out.

Grant and Taj hopped up and down, excited to explore inside the fort-palace hotel.

"Do not worry," assured Sunil, smiling at Mimi and Papa. "I will keep an eye on the children while you check in."

Grant craned his neck to stare at the giant red doors leading into the fort-palace. He tried to reach the sharp metal spikes jutting out of them but stopped when he noticed the two giant stone statues guarding the entrance.

"It looks like the entrance to a dungeon!" cried Grant. "If we go in there, we may never come out!"

"I'll go first, then," said Christina. She motioned for the others to follow. They turned right and came face to face with another, but much smaller, version of the doors they had just come through.

"Wow! This really might be a dungeon!" exclaimed Christina.

"Told you so!" returned Grant.

"Grant, over here!" called Taj. To the left was a cobblestoned path that led up to a grassy patio. Blue metal chairs and tables were placed in neat rows on the lawn.

Welcome to Neemrana

The kids raced to the edge of a low wall adorned with potted plants and knobby-trunked trees. Up and down the outside of the fort were high arched windows and terraces spilling with vegetation. The bustling town of Neemrana sprawled below.

Grant ambled over to a manmade pond where lily pads floated on top of the water.

Something white caught his eye. He knelt down by the pond and peered into the water where tiny fish darted this way and that. There, partly hidden and resting on a lily pad, was another small paper boat!

The Mystery at the Taj Mahal

12
a really cool dungeon

"Children," called Mimi through a lattice frame etched into a wall high above the terrace. "Yoo-hoo! I see you!"

"Hi, Mimi!" returned Christina, waving.

"Come on up!" shouted Papa. "We should get you kids settled in your room while there's still light. You'll want to get your bearings before dark. Otherwise, we may have four lost kids on our hands come nightfall," he warned. "Thank you, Sunil, for looking after them!"

Sunil waved and bid everyone a good night.

The kids raced up the stone steps and followed Mimi and Papa to their rooms.

Along the way, they passed a woman wearing a colorful *sari*. Behind her trotted a small boy about three years of age. The woman smiled at Christina and Mahal as she walked by.

The girls trailed behind the others. "What was that reddish spot on her forehead?" whispered Christina.

"Many people call it a *bindi*, but it also goes by other names, depending on its purpose," explained Mahal. "That woman is wearing it because it shows she's a married woman. But nowadays, many people wear it as a fashion statement."

"Do we really have to go down there?" Christina heard her brother say. He was pointing to a dark, curving staircase chiseled into the rock.

"Sure!" said Papa. "Just hang onto the rope on your way down." They descended the steep steps one at a time until they reached a dark wooden door. It creaked on its hinges when it opened.

A Really Cool Dungeon

"It *is* a dungeon!" screeched Grant. "A really cool dungeon!"

The kids stepped onto gleaming marble floors with an intricate inlaid pattern. Framed mirrors and art adorned the rough rock walls.

"We'll be next door if you need us," announced Mimi cheerfully. The kids listened to the click click click of Mimi's red high-heeled pumps going up the steps. "I'll try to get some work done before dinnertime."

"Are you ready for the next clue?" announced Grant. He pulled the newest paper boat out of his pocket.

"But, when? Where? How?" asked Christina, flustered.

"About ten minutes ago. In the garden pond. With my hand!" answered Grant.

Taj and Mahal giggled.

He unfolded the boat and read the clue.

where walls won't hold
wind dances
and cradles swing!

"Cradles?" cried Christina, looking at the others. "As in baby cradles?"

13

aankh-micholi, anyone?

The kids left their room to explore the fort-palace grounds. The smells of Indian curry drifted across the palace. The kids played on a human-sized chessboard, hopping from square to square.

Christina took in the scenery and sighed. A light breeze blew. The sun hung small and low on the horizon. Strings of lights blinked on, bringing a festive atmosphere. From the air, she thought, a passing airplane might mistake the fort-palace for a cruise ship resting on its side.

Local musicians played Rajasthan desert folk songs for dancing guests on a lower terrace.

Taj suggested playing a game of *Aankh-Micholi*, a game similar to hide-and-seek. "Except the person who is 'It' starts out wearing a blindfold," he explained.

A waiter cheerfully gave the kids a handkerchief to use as a blindfold. Grant was "It" first. Since it was getting dark, they decided to limit the hiding area to one level of the fort-palace.

They all took off in different directions. Christina's heart quickened when she heard Grant yell "Ready or not, here I come!"

Soon she got lost in the maze of outdoor halls. The further she roamed, the fainter the music got.

The paint on the outer walls of the fort-palace was chipped and darker than Christina remembered. *Maybe it was too dark to play this game,* she thought to herself. She crouched down when she heard Grant call her name.

"Taj is my prisoner!" he shouted. "You will be next!"

Aankh-Micholi, Anyone?

His voice faded and was replaced by a woman singing. Christina couldn't understand the words, but it sounded sad. She followed the voice until she came to a room with open-arched windows. A warm breeze blew in.

Swings from different times throughout India's history filled the airy room. Some hung from chains, while others balanced on wooden bases.

The singing stopped as soon as Christina stepped into the room. The faint scent of lavender hung in the air. A cradle in the far corner began to rock back and forth.

"Hello! Is anyone in here?" she asked from the door. Her voice sounded funny and hollow.

A baby cried, faintly at first, and then louder. Christina's heart raced. "I'll be back," she called from the door. She turned and ran smack into Grant.

A smile crept onto Grant's face. "You are my last prisoner!" he announced.

Taj and Mahal stood captive behind Grant.

"Cool room!" he said. He snapped his fingers. "Prisoners, you are free!"

Taj and Mahal let out a sigh of relief.

Christina's eyes lit up. "I was just coming to get you all. I heard a baby crying in that cradle over there."

They walked closer to the rocking cradle and peered inside. It wasn't a baby at all. It was a kitten!

"Ahh, Kitty! What are you doing in here?" she asked. It was so tiny and fragile and looked mournfully up at the kids with big green eyes.

Christina picked up the kitten and held her close. It purred. Just then, a little girl and boy ran up to Christina and tugged on her shirt.

"Is this your kitten?" she asked the children.

They nodded and took their kitten from Christina. "*Dhanyavaad!*" they said and hurried off to play.

"You're welcome!" responded Christina with a smile.

Grant grew wide-eyed. "The clue, Christina!"

Christina pulled it out of her backpack and read it again:

where walls won't hold
wind dances
and cradles swing!

"But, what does a kitten have to do with the clue?" she asked. What Christina really wanted to ask was why she heard a woman singing and why the cradle began to rock by itself when there was no one in the room. She decided to keep that to herself.

"I don't think it has anything to do with it," answered her brother. He studied the cradle. "Aha!" he cried. "This cradle has a fake bottom!" He pulled up the bottom to uncover a bottle overlaid in colorful jewels.

The map inside the bottle was old and the ink crumbled—just like the first one. "The map starts from this fort-palace!" announced Christina.

"And ends at some sort of arched building," added Grant. *Where would it lead them this time?*

14
into the
baoli abyss

KNOCK KNOCK!

Christina awoke to a sharp knock at the door. She stumbled over to open it.

"Good morning!" exclaimed Sunil from the doorway. "Rise and shine!"

Christina thought it was way too early to be so chipper. "Good morning," she mumbled and yawned.

"What would you children say to a camel ride after breakfast?" he asked.

In a flash, images of Christina's camel-in-the-desert dream came flooding back to her.

"Where are we going?" she asked Sunil.

"A stepwell is not far from here," he said. "Your grandparents thought you kids would enjoy seeing it. They said you liked adventure!"

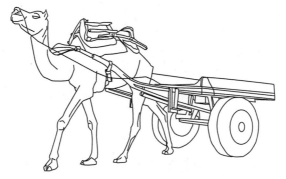

Waiting outside the gates to the Neemrana Fort-Palace stood a very tall, tan-colored camel. Its long, bony legs dwarfed the cushioned wagon on wheels attached to its back.

"We're really going on a camel ride?" asked Grant. He pumped his fist in the air. "YESSSS!"

Sunil helped the kids onto the wagon. He took the reins and led the camel into the crowded town, bustling with noise and activity.

Into the Baoli Abyss

Down an alley, the kids watched women and young girls in flowing garments balance metal urns full of water on their heads. Little children raced by in waves, chattering and laughing.

The camel came to an abrupt stop. Grant landed face first in the cushion.

"Welcome to the *baoli*," announced Sunil. "This manmade well was built over six hundred years ago!"

"Wow!" cried Grant, rubbing his sore nose. "This barrel is a well?! This is one giant barrel, that's for sure!"

"*Baoli*," corrected Sunil, laughing. "Not barrel!"

Christina leaned over and peered down into the deep well. The enormous underground structure had one above-ground floor, with the remaining nine floors descending into a deep, dark **abyss**. "It looks like an underground apartment building!" she cried.

"Mr. Sunil, do you know many steps there are to the bottom?" asked Grant.

"About 200," he answered. "It's probably bone dry down there these days."

The kids examined the levels they could see. Each of the stone arched levels seemed to be a mirror image of the one below it.

"The arched building!" whispered Christina to Grant.

"The map clue!" he whispered back.

"Sunil, may we explore?" she asked.

Sunil nodded. "Just be careful!" he added with a stern tone they hadn't heard before. "The steps going down are very wobbly!"

The kids descended the steps into darkness. The deeper they got, the mustier and older the air smelled.

Once they reached the bottom, Grant celebrated. "WHOO HOO!" he cried. "This is so cool! I wonder if anyone lives down here."

"Grant! Don't say things like that!" cried his sister.

COO COO!

"Grant, stop that!" she yelled. "I know it's you!"

COO COO!

"Stop it!" she demanded.

"It wasn't me!" shouted Grant. He stamped his foot. A poof of dust sprung up from the dirty floor. Flapping wings followed. Then, more flapping. Christina screamed and crouched, pulling Mahal down with her. The boys took off running through the darkness.

"Grant! Taj!" called Christina. "Come back!" Her voice echoed in the dark space. "Do you hear them?" she asked Mahal.

"No, nothing," she answered.

Christina was sick with fear. "We have to find them! What if there's another well, one we don't know about?"

The girls made their way through the darkness, arms stretched out in front of them.

A voice whispered softly in a language Christina could not understand. The voice grew louder. Christina froze.

"Christina!" screeched Mahal. "Christina, where did you go?"

"Mahal! I'm here!" answered Christina. "Did you hear her voice?"

"What are you talking about? What voice? Christina, I'm scared!" whimpered Mahal.

"There it is again," said Christina. The voice was velvety-soft and faint.

"I heard her!" cried Mahal. "She's telling us to stop running."

"What else is she saying?" asked Christina.

"She's telling us not to be afraid!" said her friend.

"Do you smell that?" asked Christina.

"Lavender?" wondered Mahal.

"Lavender!" exclaimed Christina.

"Boo!" shouted Grant.

Christina and Mahal were beyond being startled by Grant's trick. All they felt was relief that their brothers were OK.

"The map, Christina. Do you have it?" asked Grant.

"Oh, I almost forgot!" she said. "It won't do any good, though. It's too dark to see anything."

Christina pulled the map out of her backpack and unrolled it. The map that the kids had seen near the cradle was no longer visible. In its place was a lavender-colored etching of the *baoli*.

"Glow-in-the-dark ink?" asked Grant.

"Yes!" said Christina, moving the map up and down.

"See the rectangular shape of this building?" asked Taj.

"And the three crowns make the shape of a triangle!" exclaimed Mahal.

"The first crown is by the entrance," said Christina. The kids hurried to where the steps met the bottom floor. A faint bit of light filtered down to them.

"The next crown is down a bit," said Mahal.

"I'll go," said Grant bravely.

"Maybe you don't have to," said Christina. "We should be able to figure this out." With her finger, she drew imaginary lines. "The lines intersect here!" she said.

The kids walked several steps and stopped. "It's so dark down here!" Christina exclaimed. She reached out and slid her hand up the smooth surface of an arched wall until she reached the top.

"There's another small door!" she cried. She slid the wooden door open and carefully reached inside the hollowed-out arch.

"You guys, I found another pouch!" she cried. But this one was much larger and heavier than the last one. She slid it into her backpack and scurried with the others up the stairs and into the blinding summer sun.

15

trapped!

At dinner that evening, Papa announced, "Tomorrow morning, Mr. Sunil will drive us to the city of Mathura, where we'll take the Shatabdi Express train to the city of Agra."

Christina's face brightened. "The Taj Mahal is in Agra!" she stated, scooping up savory vegetable curry with a piece of *nan*, a flat, buttery Indian bread.

"Christina, only the right hand!" Mahal reminded her. "Remember, that's how people in India eat their food."

Christina nodded. She put her left hand back in her lap and tried to keep from pushing the food off her plate. She looked over at Grant and was shocked to see how well he performed this balancing act.

"We'll be up at the crack of dawn," boomed Papa. "That means lights out at nine tonight. No exceptions!"

That night, in their room, everyone piled onto Christina's bed to examine their new treasure. The cream-colored pouch had a golden clasp, just like the first one. This time, though, it was filled with at least twice the number of pearls.

Christina grew pensive. "These pearls look very old and very expensive!"

Grant nodded. "So do the pouches!"

Christina placed the smaller pouch next to the new one. The pouches and pearls shimmered in the soft light of the table lamp.

"The material used to make both pouches looks the same," noted Mahal.

"I wonder if they were cut from the same cloth," said Christina. She ran her fingers across the pouches and felt notches in the fabric. To Christina, they looked like tiny puncture holes.

Trapped!

Just then, the door to their room screeched open. The kids' eyes darted to the curtain that separated them from the main room.

Christina quickly scooped the pearls back into the pouches and slipped them into her backpack.

"It's past nine!" she whispered. "We're supposed to be asleep!"

Grant whispered back. "If it were Papa, he would have said something by now." Grant moved to switch off the light, but Christina stopped him. "They'll see the light go off!"

Grant nodded and motioned for the kids to follow him through the woven curtain that separated his room from Christina's. He pointed to a rock wall above his bed. Where normally a painting would hang, there was a curtain that hid a hollowed out wall with a metal cage door.

The kids looked at Grant like he'd been keeping a secret from them. He shrugged and opened the rusty cage gate. "Help me up!" he whispered.

After everyone squeezed into the nook, Christina closed the cage gate shut behind her and reached through the metal bars to close the curtain. Then, they waited.

Outside the cramped space, they heard two sets of footsteps and two voices, a man's and a woman's.

"I'm sure they found something by now! Where could they have hidden it?" the woman hissed.

Christina recognized the voice immediately as that of the flight attendant.

"We should go. They might come back!" the man warned in a rolling British accent. The voice sounded vaguely familiar to Christina. Through a slit in the curtain, she saw the flight attendant. Standing next to her was a man wearing a dark brown turban. His back was turned to her.

"They're just kids!" the woman said.

"We can't risk getting caught!" he argued.

BANG!

"Someone's coming!" said the woman. "We have to hide!"

Trapped!

"Quick! In the other room!" whispered the man.

"Christina! Grant!" roared Papa from the front room. "Taj! Mahal! You in here?"

"We're in here!" they shouted.

Christina tried to push the gate open, but the outside latch had closed, locking them in. "We're over here, Papa!" She squeezed her hand through the bars again and managed to yank the curtain open so Papa could find them.

Papa hurried into the room. "How in the world did you get stuck in there?" he asked. "Good thing I came to check on you. Your room door was wide open!"

16

all aboard the shatabdi express!

"All aboard the Shatabdi Express!" roared Papa from the train car. "We made it just in the nick of time!"

"Is this the train that takes us to the Taj Mahal?" asked Grant.

"Pretty close to it," answered Mimi. "The Shatabdi is the fastest train in India, so we should reach Agra in just under an hour."

The kids shared a table seat, with the boys on one side and the girls on the other. "You do realize you and Taj will be riding in reverse the whole trip, don't you?" Christina warned Grant.

The boys looked at each other and bumped fists. "Cool!" they exclaimed.

Outside the window, the Indian countryside unfolded like the pages in a picture book. Christina felt nervous seeing pedestrians and animals walking so close to their speeding train. She brought her feet up to her seat and hid her face in her knees.

Just then, she heard the squeaking sound of wheels turning. "Snacks, traditional Indian snacks!" announced a woman in a voice that Christina recognized.

Christina leaned her head back and looked up. A mirror ran the length of the underside of the luggage rack above her.

"Snacks," repeated the woman in a sing-song voice. "Traditional Indian snacks!" She passed by Christina and Mahal.

In the mirror, Christina saw an arm reach across the table and place a bag of chips in front of Taj and another in front of Grant. Curly Sanskrit lettering decorated the bags.

"Snacks, traditional Indian snacks!" the woman continued.

"The snacks are free?" asked Grant.

Christina leaned into the aisle and watched a passenger stop the woman, pay for a snack, and receive change in return.

"Miss!" called Christina from her seat. "We didn't pay for the snacks!"

The woman stiffened and turned her head slightly, then continued forward.

SCREEEECH! Grant slapped his hands over his ears to drown out the high-pitched sound of metal grinding against metal.

"Hold on!" boomed Papa. "Looks like we're stopping!"

The passengers lurched forward as the train ground to a halt, then rushed to look out the windows.

A young boy with his head shaved and wearing a reddish purple robe stayed seated. He continued to read his book. "Cows on the tracks," he announced without looking up.

"Did we hit them?" asked Grant.

"Perhaps yes, perhaps no," he answered.

"I hope not," said Christina.

"Being alone, one has only one's thoughts to consider," he said, nodding his head.

"Excuse me?" said Christina.

The boy was quiet. He set his book down and closed his eyes.

Christina turned and realized that Grant was gone. She raced to the window and saw her brother caught in a swarm of people gawking at the cattle blocking the train.

Then, she saw two familiar faces, those of Taj and Mahal, hurry up behind Grant and yank him out of the crowd.

Mahal waved to Christina and pointed to Grant. "He's OK!" she seemed to say.

Christina waved and shouted through the open window, "Are Mimi and Papa outside?"

Mahal put her hand to her ear.

"She can't hear you," said the boy.

Christina turned and looked carefully at the young boy sitting so calmly. "You didn't see my grandparents, did you?" she asked.

With his eyes still closed, he answered, "I didn't see them get off the train, if that's what you want to know."

Suddenly, Christina felt abandoned. "OK. Thank you," she said.

"Beware of the one who leaves the clues," he whispered. "You recognized her voice, didn't you?"

Christina's eyes grew wide. "How did you know that?"

The boy seemed to have fallen asleep.

"Thank you!" she whispered.

The boy nodded.

The Mystery at the Taj Mahal

17
left behind

Christina hurried outside to meet the others in front of a makeshift store. RING! RING! RING! A man on a bicycle whooshed in front of her, barely missing her feet. She was still shaking as she told the others what had happened on the train and about the boy's warning.

"Do you think the flight attendant is following us around India," asked Mahal, "because of what a little boy said on the train?"

"That lady's voice sounded really familiar," said Christina. "Mahal, the boy knew things... things that I was thinking!"

Mahal nodded.

Grant and Taj listened intently to the conversation while munching on their chips.

Taj pointed to the sky. "It looks like it may rain," he warned. "Grant! Stop!"

Grant froze mid-chip.

"You were about to eat a piece of paper!" cried Taj.

Grant looked down at his fingers and snapped his mouth shut.

"It's a paper boat!" exclaimed Christina. "And it was in your chip bag!"

Grant's eyes grew wide. "No wonder it was free!" he exclaimed.

He unfolded the boat and read the message:

> the charmer holds the secret
> reflections conceal
> a covering at last returned!

The kids hadn't noticed that the swarms of people had thinned. They hadn't noticed that the cattle had been coaxed off the track. They hadn't even noticed that the train was leaving without them!

Left Behind

Christina thought of the boy on the train and his warning. She looked up just as the train was leaving. The boy rested his forehead against the window, watching them. She glimpsed Mimi and Papa walking back and forth on the train.

Christina fumbled for her phone. "They're probably trying to call me right now!"

For a fleeting second, Christina had the feeling that she was on one page of a picture book, and the next page was about to turn without her.

"He knew we were going to miss the train!" cried Christina. "He didn't have to leave us behind!"

"I think we got ourselves left behind," said Grant matter-of-factly.

"The boy is probably a practicing Buddhist," explained Mahal. "They believe we are born with a predetermined destiny, a karma. He probably thought that even if he had warned us, whatever was supposed to happen would eventually happen anyway."

"Then, why did he warn me about the one who leaves the clues?" wondered Christina.

"Maybe it was part of his destiny to warn you," guessed Taj, shrugging his shoulders.

"Well, I hope our destiny takes us to Agra!" cried Christina. "Any ideas?"

"We can always take the bus," suggested Mahal.

"You have money?" asked Christina.

Mahal smiled. "My dad gave me some for emergencies just like this!"

18

a roof
with a view

"When you said we would take a bus, I never imagined you meant like this!" exclaimed Grant, smiling.

The four kids sat side by side on top of a rickety old bus that clicked as it moved down the crowded road. Several men, some luggage, and a sheep in a small crate joined them.

Mahal smiled a crooked grin. "The bus was full! At least they let us on, right?"

Grant smiled. "Who knows? Maybe you'll have better phone reception up here," he joked.

The kids enjoyed the trip to Agra on top of the bus, even with the endless stops and **incessant** honking. Christina took pictures with her cell phone in between unsuccessful calls to Mimi and Papa.

Christina quickly flipped through the images she'd already taken. Among the snapshots of storefronts, free-roaming cattle and wild boar, shacks stacked on top of each other, and trucks and buses so close you could touch them, were throngs of people everywhere.

Christina wished Mimi and Papa were there with them, not because she was scared, but because she wanted to share with them the thrill of riding on top of a bus in the middle of a country she barely knew or understood.

Christina leaned forward to look at the other kids. Above the din of the blaring traffic noises, she shouted, "Maybe this is what the boy knew we should experience!"

"Christina, you just got a text!" shouted Grant, pointing to the tiny message displayed on her phone.

"It's from Mimi!" she shouted. "She says not to worry! She says the boy says hello and to take a bus!"

Christina texted back. "Tell the boy he was right not to warn us! And we're on a bus! See you in Agra!" She snapped a photo of the four of them and sent it on with the text.

The Mystery at the Taj Mahal

19

the old
snake charmer

The kids ran to the bus stop bathrooms to wash up, while Mimi and Papa hired drivers to take them to the Taj Mahal on battery-powered rickshaws called *tuk-tuks*.

The girls emerged from the bathroom to find their brothers sitting cross-legged in the grass. Across from them sat a very old man with a long, scraggly white beard that reached to his lap. He wore a red speckled turban, an orange cotton shirt, and billowing white pants that hugged his ankles.

Between them was a basket with the name "Charlie" sewn into the front.

Grant waved to the girls and patted the ground next to him. "Sit," he instructed. "He's got a snake named Charlie!"

Mahal smiled. "He's a snake charmer!" she whispered.

Christina said, "The clue, remember?!"

The old man reached out and removed the top of the basket. He blew into an instrument that was part flute and part gourd. The sound reminded Christina of bagpipes, only softer.

The kids leaned back and laughed nervously when a massive cobra rose out of the basket, swaying back and forth. When the snake charmer stopped to take a short breath, Charlie lunged and hissed at him.

The Old Snake Charmer

The snake charmer slowly brought the top of the basket down over the cobra's head, coaxing it back inside. Then he ran his knobby, weathered hand over the basket's cover and began to chant in a sing-song voice.

Mahal's jaw dropped. She leaned in and whispered, "He's chanting some of the words Shah Jahan used to describe the Taj Mahal. He's saying, 'Should a sinner make his way to this mansion, all his past sins are to be washed away. The sight of this mansion creates sorrowing sighs; and the sun and moon shed tears from their eyes.'"

When the old man finished chanting, he gestured to Christina to open the basket. Despite her fear of snakes, Christina mustered up the courage. She reached over and quickly lifted the cover.

The old man gasped. He stood up, stumbled backward several feet, and toppled to the ground. Grant and Taj ran to help him up.

"What's wrong?" Christina asked. She carefully peeked inside the basket. Charlie was gone! In his place was a bottle adorned with colorful jewels!

Two red doorless *tuk-tuks* pulled up to the curb. Papa called to the children from the backseat of the *tuk-tuk* in front. "We gotta get moving!" he roared. "Storm's approaching!"

Thunder rumbled and a cool wind picked up the scent of lavender.

For a brief second, the woman in robes stood across the busy street. Then she was gone! Christina plucked the bottle out of Charlie's basket and slipped it into her backpack. They raced to their *tuk-tuk* and hopped inside.

"Change of plans!" called Papa. "We're heading for Agra Fort to wait out the storm!"

"OK!" they hollered back, huddling close in their seats.

20

on to

agra fort

In the back of the *tuk-tuk,* the kids chatted excitedly about the snake charmer

"Do you think it was magic?" asked Taj.

"The old man looked pretty shocked!" laughed Grant. "I don't think he expected his pet cobra Charlie to disappear like that!"

Christina looked back to see the old man reunited with his cobra. His face lit up with a toothless grin.

Christina smiled and leaned in. "Listen! I saw the woman in robes again."

"It's probably the flight attendant trying to spook you!" exclaimed Grant.

"I'm not so sure about that," she answered. She thought about the scent of lavender being linked to the bottle clues.

"What do you mean?" asked Grant.

"I think the person who is leaving the paper clues is different from the one leaving the bottles," she answered.

"What I don't understand," said Mahal, "is why the flight attendant, if that's who's doing it, is leaving the clues at all!"

"Yeah," agreed Taj. "If she has the clues, then why doesn't she just try to solve the mystery herself?"

"Maybe she can't," answer Christina. "Maybe she needs someone to help her."

"Why did she pick you two to figure out the mystery?" asked Mahal.

"You mean us, right?" said Christina with a smile.

"Us," agreed Mahal.

On to Agra Fort

"I think the flight attendant heard me talking to your dad about always getting mixed up in mysteries," explained Christina.

"I bet that flight attendant is a jewel thief!" said Grant.

"Why do you say that?" asked Taj.

"She had a bag full of jeweled bottles stuffed in the airplane," said Grant.

Christina winced. She knew Mahal's father exported bottles like the ones she saw in the bag. "Grant, we don't know that for sure. They could have been anything!"

Mahal and Taj looked at each other and grew quiet.

"I just realized something," said Christina, trying to change the subject. "This is the first time we've found the bottle before finishing the paper clue!"

She pulled it out and read:

the charmer holds the secret
reflections conceal
a covering at last returned!

"You're right!" agreed Grant. "We've solved the "charmer" part of the clue, but not the last two lines."

"Maybe we don't need the last part of the clue," said Mahal. "We've already found the bottle clue."

Christina opened the bottle and unrolled the map. As before, the map was drawn with a chalky purple and gold ink.

"It's the Agra Fort! I'm sure of it!" cried Mahal. "See the wall that surrounds the fort? And these simple lines represent the palaces and towers within the fort's walls."

"Palaces? Towers?" said Christina. "It sounds like a place of fairytales!"

"The Agra Fort has a long history. By the time Emperor Akra ruled, it was nearly in ruins.

On to Agra Fort

He and his grandson, Shah Jahan, completely rebuilt it."

"Shah Jahan? The Shah Jahan that built the Taj Mahal?" asked Christina.

"Yes," said Mahal. "In fact, the Taj Mahal and Agra Fort are only about two kilometers apart."

As their *tuk-tuks* rounded a bend in the road, rain began to fall in sheets. Through the downpour, the reddish-brown outline of the Agra Fort emerged, only it wasn't small and pencil thin like on the map. The thick walls towered above them, making the kids feel very small.

21

the reflecting pool

Once inside the walls of Agra Fort, Grant whispered to the other kids, "There are so many buildings and passageways! How will we ever know where to look?"

"Yeah," agreed Taj. "This is more like a walled city than a fort!"

Mimi and Papa were studying the brochure and admiring the architecture.

Christina pulled out the map.

"Your hair!" cried Grant. "It's dripping on the map!"

Christina gasped and quickly shook the map of the excess water. She set it on a low wall.

"The map is still running!" exclaimed Grant.

Christina shook her head. "No, it's moving on its own!"

The aerial view of Agra Fort started to fade on the map and was replaced by what looked to be the layout of one room etched in golden purple ink. Curled lines and three crowns appeared below one swift stroke of ink.

"This time the map reacted to water!" noted Mahal with a smile.

"It's magical!" cried Christina.

Taj pointed at the changing map. "This room could be anywhere!"

"Whatever we do, we'd better do it fast. The image is fading," squealed Christina.

Grant sprinkled some water on the map. The room reappeared briefly, then began fading again.

Christina looked worried. "Is there a place in Agra Fort that is more important than any other?"

Taj and Mahal looked at each other. "Yes!" they shouted.

Mahal glanced at the map in the brochure. "Come on!" she called. "Follow me!"

The Reflecting Pool

Mimi and Papa had meandered ahead of the kids. "What's so special about the room?" asked Christina as they hurried down covered outdoor corridors decorated with intricate designs.

"It's where Shah Jahan was imprisoned by his son!" explained Mahal.

Christina's eyes grew wide. "Imprisoned by his own son?"

"Yes!" she said. "He was put under house arrest in the same tower he had built for his wife before her death."

Grant looked shocked. "He locked his own wife in a tower? What kind of family was that!?"

"No, of course not," said Mahal. "Wait until you see this tower. When Shah Jahan had the tower built, it wasn't used to lock anyone away!"

Grant asked, "Why was the shah imprisoned?"

Taj explained, "Sometime after the Taj Mahal was built, Shah Jahan became very ill. His sons vied for position to become the next emperor. One of the sons took over by force and imprisoned his father!"

"We're here!" announced Mahal.

"You're right!" cried Christina. "It is beautiful!"

Christina waved to Mimi and Papa. They smiled and waved back.

The kids entered the multi-storied, marble-domed tower. It was adorned with inlaid precious stones, marble latticework, an outdoor veranda with a fountain, and breathtaking views of the Yamuna River and the Taj Mahal. The marble floors glistened.

"Christina, what's wrong?" asked Grant.

His sister frowned. "I can't tell if the map is upside down, sideways, or right side up!"

"This long line is most likely the Yamuna River," said Mahal.

Christina turned the map around. "OK, but the crowns don't match up with the room at all."

Grant turned in a giant circle and puffed out his chest. "If I were emperor, I would have a secret place where I could go. I would keep my most prized possessions there. And only a select few of my most trusted allies and family would know about it!"

"That's exactly what Shah Jahan did!" exclaimed Mahal. "Come look!" Mahal led them outside onto the terrace. She pointed to the Yamuna River and to the Taj Mahal in the distance.

"The Yamuna River also flows behind the Taj Mahal," she said. "After Shah Jahan's wife, Mumtaz, died, he was so heartbroken that he wanted to build something so beautiful that her death would be remembered forever."

Taj added, "The Taj Mahal is actually a **mausoleum**. When it was completed, Shah Jahan had his wife's body interred in a tomb inside the Taj Mahal."

Mahal was excited to explain what else she knew about the Taj Mahal. "There is a legend," she explained, "that Shah Jahan wanted to build a black Taj Mahal, an exact replica, directly across from the white Taj Mahal."

"I guess he never had a chance to build it, being locked up and all!" remarked Grant.

"Some scientists," she added, "now believe that he never planned to make a replica because they found the remains of a secret garden and a reflecting pool instead. Shah Jahan most likely invited only his closest allies and friends to visit the reflecting pool. Can you guess what they saw on moonlit nights reflected in the water?"

Christina gasped. "A black Taj Mahal!"

"Exactly!" Mahal exclaimed.

"Christina," said Grant. "What was the second line of the paper clue?"

Christina looked at the clue. "It says 'reflections conceal.'"

"We are looking in the wrong place for the treasure. Look!" Grant shouted. "That wall is reflected on the marble floor!"

The kids knelt down on the floor. "The crowns on the map should be here, here, and here," noted Christina, pointing to the wall.

Grant and Taj found the corresponding reflections on the floor.

"Then, the center point would be here," said Mahal.

Grant pressed down on a small section of the marble floor. The tile rose and shifted to the right. The kids cheered when it opened.

Christina reached in and pulled out another silk pouch, twice the size of the second one. Inside were exquisite, glistening pearls!

Grant slid the tile back in place.

Christina put her finger to her lips. "I hear someone coming!" she whispered. "And she sounds mad!" Christina motioned for everyone to follow her into an adjoining chamber, where she found ornately adorned arching pillars, but nowhere to hide. They leaned against a pillar. CREAK! Something shifted.

Christina realized they were leaning on a hidden door in the pillar itself. The kids slid through the door and nudged it closed. Through the marble lattice, they could hear two people and make out their shapes.

"We've checked every nook and cranny of this fort for those kids!" the woman hissed. "I've invested too much time and effort into finding this treasure to let it slip through my fingers now!"

"Why haven't you tried to find it yourself?" asked the man.

"Believe me, I've tried! I don't understand how they've gotten this far," the woman exclaimed. "It's almost like they're getting help."

Christina looked at the others, wide-eyed in the dim cavern.

"I know you want to be famous for finding this lost treasure, but maybe—" began the man.

"I want fame *and* fortune!" she interrupted.

The man shook his fist in frustration. "But what you're trying to find is a national treasure!" he cried. "You can't have both fame and fortune—only one or the other!"

The woman ran her hand over the carved marble of the pillar where the kids were hiding. They leaned back and covered their mouths so she couldn't hear them breathe.

"Anyway, why are you so sure this treasure even exists?" he asked.

The woman turned to the man. "Five years of research in old dusty libraries tell me so!" she countered.

CLICK!

"What was that?" she asked. She ran her hand over the marble column again and pushed against its side. She grinned and looked at the man as a door arched open.

22
a sparkling
taj mahal

"Judging from the smiles on your faces, you kids had a good ol' time!" boomed Papa.

Everyone piled into two red, battery-powered *tuk-tuks,* and their drivers sped toward the Taj Mahal. The kids traveled in one vehicle, while Mimi and Papa rode in another just behind them.

"Phew!" Taj exclaimed. "I can't believe we got out of that place in one piece!"

"Thanks to Grant," Christina said, proud of her little brother. While the kids were trapped in the pillar, Grant had bumped into a lever that opened to reveal an escape route—a narrow set of marble steps that led one floor down. "You know," she added, "your clumsiness comes in handy sometimes!"

Grant laughed and nodded.

Mahal pointed and shouted over the deafening Agra traffic. "That's the Yamuna River, the one we saw from the tower! See? There's the Taj Mahal on the banks of the river!"

Christina nodded. "The reflection in the water really is just as beautiful!"

Mahal nodded fervently. "I think so, too!"

Everyone fell silent as they took in the sheer size and beauty of the mausoleum, even from this distance.

Christina suddenly felt compelled to sketch the Taj Mahal and its reflection in the Yamuna River. She left nothing out of her drawing: a sparkling dome that seemed to reach the sky; two much smaller arched domes to its right and left; four towers, two in the front and two in the back, jutting up from each corner of the high stone wall surrounding the structure. As she drew in her notebook, Christina wondered how Mimi must be feeling seeing the Taj Mahal for the first time.

Once they reached the no-car zone surrounding the Taj Mahal, the traffic noises virtually disappeared. Christina asked Taj and Mahal, "What did the flight attendant mean back there about a treasure?"

"Some things were stolen from the Taj Mahal over the years, especially during the British Raj," explained Mahal.

Taj added, "Other things, like diamonds inlaid in the tomb or a pearl blanket that was supposedly laid over Mumtaz Mahal's tomb were—"

"Wait!" interrupted Christina. "Did you say a 'pearl blanket'?"

"Yes," said Mahal. "But it's only a legend."

"Hmmm. Last night, I noticed notches in the fabric of the pouches," said Christina. "I wonder if the pearls might have been attached to the material at one time."

"But the legend said it was a pearl blanket, not pouches," said Mahal.

"If I were trying to protect a national treasure," began Christina, "especially if a world power just took over my country, I would want to hide it. And what better way to do that than to break it up into small parts?"

"So, you think the pearls were removed from the blanket and then the silk blanket was divided up to make pouches to hold the pearls?" asked Mahal.

"If it's true, it fits the clue," said Taj.

Christina read the clue one last time:

the charmer holds the secret
reflections conceal
a covering at last returned!

A Sparkling Taj Mahal

"We need to get this blanket back to its rightful owner!" exclaimed Grant.

The *tuk-tuk* driver shouted and pointed at the approaching Taj Mahal. In a rolling British accent, he said, "You want to know why the Taj Mahal doesn't get swept away in the river?" he asked.

The kids thought he was about to tell a joke. "No! Why?" they asked, smiling.

"It's because the engineers at the time dug many deep wells and filled them with rocks first. Then, they built a solid foundation on top of that. The Taj Mahal hasn't shifted very much in the past 350 years because of smart engineering!"

"Is it pure marble?" asked Grant.

The man shook his head no. "It was made of stone and brick first. The dome started out as rings of brick. Then marble and precious and semiprecious stones were inlaid. That's why the Taj Mahal sparkles!" he explained. "In fact, the white marble that covers the Taj Mahal changes color! It glistens silver on a moonlit night, pink just as the sun is about to come up, and as the sun sets, the Taj Mahal bursts with color!"

"I think it's the most beautiful building I've ever seen," said Christina.

"One more thing!" he continued. "My challenge to you when we get there is to find the two things in the entire mausoleum that are asymmetrical. Everything else is an exact mirror image!"

The kids thanked the driver for everything. After pulling into the parking lot, he turned to the kids and said, "I think what you are about to do is a very brave thing!"

"Sunil!" they shouted. "You were driving this whole time?"

He smiled brightly and led the kids to Mimi and Papa's *tuk-tuk* just as they were getting out.

"Sunil! What a surprise!" cried Mimi.

Suddenly, a woman rushed toward them, carrying a giant black bag with the initials MM etched on the side.

Just as the woman was about to reach them, Sunil nodded to three men in grey business suits standing nearby. One of the men stepped in front of her.

"Excuse me, Miss," said one of the undercover officers. "We need to have a word with you."

The flight attendant tried to escape but was intercepted by the other men.

"Excuse me, sirs," said Christina stepping forward. "May I?"

Sunil nodded to the men who relaxed their grip on the woman's arm.

"You?" she said to Sunil. "I thought you were my friend!"

"I had to protect these children!" he answered.

To Christina, she said, "Just tell me one thing," she pleaded. "What did the clues lead you to?"

"We think it's the pearl blanket that covered Mumtaz Mahal's tomb," answered Christina. "We're going to give it back to its rightful owner!"

"It's mine!" wailed the woman. "I spent five years of my life researching and searching! I deserve it!"

Christina asked, "Did you leave the paper boat clues?"

"Yes!" she hissed. "After I heard you on the airplane talking to that man about your sleuthing skills, I thought your little brother here couldn't resist a paper boat!"

Grant glared at the woman.

"Did you also leave the maps?" asked Christina.

"Those old maps?" she sputtered. "I found those in a dusty old library. I knew they led to those places, but I never could figure out where to look once I got there!"

Christina thought about the sun, the dark, and the water changing the maps. "And the bottles?" asked Christina.

The woman sneered. "I knew you couldn't resist a pretty bottle!"

"They led to some pretty scary places!" exclaimed Grant. "But we were brave!"

"But, how?" she wailed. "How did you figure out where the treasure was?" She lunged toward Christina, but Papa stepped between them.

Sunil nodded to the men as they led the woman to a nearby police station for questioning.

A Sparkling Taj Mahal

"How did you know what was happening?" Christina asked Sunil.

Sunil got serious. "I noticed a woman following you around back at the Imperial Hotel. I became alarmed and trailed her. I felt I needed to protect you children."

Christina nodded and smiled.

"I pretended to befriend her to learn more. She was intent on finding something—something that she thought *you* could find!" Sunil chuckled. "You four are quite the sleuths, that's for certain!"

"Then, it was you with her in our hotel room and at the Agra Fort, right?" asked Grant.

"It was," admitted Sunil. "You know, she stayed pretty close, but she was always a step behind."

"What do you mean?" asked Grant.

Sunil led them into the center of the mausoleum. Two tombs raised on marble platforms were laid side by side, one small and the other much bigger and off center.

"The clues couldn't have been enough to solve the mystery," he said. "How did you do it?" he asked.

The scent of lavender floated over to Christina. "Good timing, I guess," she said. "And a little help from a friend."

"Oooh! Oooh!" cried Grant, jumping up and down.

"Grant! This is a mausoleum. You can't yell in here!" chided Christina.

"Sorry!" whispered Grant. "I know the answer to the challenge question! The only things in the Taj Mahal that are not symmetrical are the tombs of the emperor and his wife!"

Christina, Grant, and their friends stood in front of the tombs surrounded by ornately carved marble screens, inlaid with gemstones that sparkled like sequins on a dancer's costume.

With Sunil translating, Christina and the kids safely returned the pearls and pouches to Taj Mahal officials.

The expressions on the officials' faces ranged from disbelief to shock to gratitude as they learned the details of the kids' adventure.

A Sparkling Taj Mahal

But their adventure wasn't over yet! A few days later, everyone was invited back to the Taj Mahal for a special ceremony.

As Papa, Mimi, Mr. Hawke, and Sunil watched, the kids each took a corner of the pearl blanket, restored to its original beauty, and carefully laid it on top of Mumtaz Mahal's upper tomb.

The scent of lavender wafted into the room. Christina noticed this time that the robed lady didn't appear to her.

Christina sighed. *Finally, the empress is at peace—in one of the most gorgeous buildings in the world—the Taj Mahal.*

the end

About the Author

Carole Marsh is an author and publisher who has written many works of fiction and non-fiction for young readers. She travels throughout the United States and around the world to research her books. In 1979, Carole Marsh was named Communicator of the Year for her corporate communications work with major national and international corporations.

Marsh is the founder and CEO of Gallopade International, established in 1979. Today, Gallopade International is widely recognized as a leading source of educational materials for every state and many countries. Marsh and Gallopade were recipients of the 2004 Teachers' Choice Award. Marsh has written more than 50 Carole Marsh Mysteries™. In 2007, she was named Georgia Author of the Year. Years ago, her children, Michele and Michael, were the original characters in her mystery books. Today, they continue the Carole Marsh Books tradition by working at Gallopade. By adding grandchildren Grant and Christina as new mystery characters, she has continued the tradition for a third generation.

Ms. Marsh welcomes correspondence from her readers. You can e-mail her at fanclub@gallopade.com, visit carolemarshmysteries.com, or write to her in care of Gallopade International, P.O. Box 2779, Peachtree City, Georgia, 30269 USA.

Built-In Book Club

talk about it!

1. Have you, or anyone in your family, ever experienced jet lag? If so, explain what jet lag is and how it affects people.

2. The *boalis* were used as wells. There is talk that the Neemrana *baoli*, which is over 600 years old, is to be converted into a bazaar where people can sell their goods. Do you think that is a good or bad idea? Defend your opinion.

3. Discuss the significance of the lavender scent in the story. What is happening when a character smells the scent of lavender?

4. Scientists believe that Moghul Emperor Shah Jahan never intended to build a black Taj Mahal. Use information from the story to back this claim. What do you think?

5. Would you like to travel to India? Why or why not? If your answer is yes, what would you like to see there?

6. India has the second-highest population in the world. What country has the highest population? What are some problems that could arise in a country with an extremely high population?

7. Who is your favorite character in the mystery? Explain why.

8. Think about some of the unusual means of transportation experienced by the kids in the mystery. Which would you prefer—riding in a camel cart or on top of a bus? Why?

Built-In Book Club

bring it to life!

1. Map it! Find India on a world map. Draw India and the countries surrounding it on a poster board. Label India, its neighbors, and any bodies of water near it. What continent is India part of? Label the continent.

2. The Moghul Empire produced some of India's most beautiful architecture. Use the Internet to find photographs of the buildings mentioned in the mystery. Print the photos and display them on a poster. Which building is your favorite?

3. Choose a room or place at Neemrana Fort Palace. It could be the human-sized chessboard, the cradle hall, or the cage in the kids' room. Write your own scene in that place. Include as many mystery characters as you can.

4. Cows are sacred in India. Research how they are treated in India, and write a story titled "A Day in My Life" from an Indian cow's point of view.

5. What's the weather like in Delhi, India? Research the average temperatures, month by month, in Delhi, India. Then, research the average monthly temperatures where you live. Create a chart comparing the two places. Do you prefer the weather in India or where you live?

6. Bring in a guest speaker! Do you know anyone from India? If so, ask him or her to speak to your group about what life is like in India. Be sure to listen closely and ask lots of questions. That's the best way to learn!

taj mahal trivia

1. Mughal Emperor Shah Jahan designed the Taj Mahal and had it built in memory of his third wife, Mumtaz Mahal, who died giving birth to their fourteenth child.

2. The Taj Mahal is over 350 years old. Construction of the mausoleum began in 1632 and took 22 years to complete.

3. Over 1,000 elephants were used to help transport materials used to make the Taj Mahal.

4. The main dome of the Taj Mahal is over ten stories high, is completely unsupported by pillars, and has over 30 precious and semi-precious stones inlaid in the marble covering the outside of the dome.

5. Calligraphy, which cites the Quran, can be found carved into the stone of the Taj Mahal.

6. The Taj Mahal is completely symmetrical, except for Shah Jahan's tomb, which was placed in the Taj Mahal after his death.

7. The Taj Mahal takes on different colors depending on the time of day.

8. Many of the descendants of the hundreds of artisans that worked on the Taj Mahal are still actively carving things today, like furniture and jewelry boxes.

9. Once construction of the Taj Mahal was complete, Emperor Shah Jahan became ill. He was put under house arrest in the Agra Fort by one of his sons, who forcefully took over the role of emperor.

10. During recent wars, scaffolding was used to cover the dome of the Taj Mahal to protect it from bombings from the air.

glossary

 **abyss:** a deep or seemingly bottomless hole or opening in the earth

 **altitude:** the height of an object or point in relation to sea level or ground level

chaos: complete disorder and confusion

disembark: get off a plane, train, or ship

dwarfed: made something else look small in comparison

 **incessant:** continuing for a long time without stopping

interred: placed in a grave or tomb

Glossary

SAT **mausoleum:** a large tomb or a building that houses tombs

nook: a recess or corner in a room

SAT **pedestrian:** someone who is traveling on foot

pensive: thinking deeply about something

predetermined: decided in advance

sari: the traditional dress of women, mainly in India and Pakistan, consisting of a very long narrow piece of cloth elaborately swathed around the body

searing: very strong

simian: relating to apes and monkeys

urn: a large vase

Visit the <u>carolemarshmysteries.com</u> website to:

- Join the Carole Marsh Mysteries™ Fan Club!

- Write a letter to Christina, Grant, Mimi, or Papa!

- Cast your vote for where the next mystery should take place!

- Find fascinating facts about the countries where the mysteries take place!

- Track your reading on an international map!

- Take the Fact or Fiction online quiz!

- Find out where the Mystery Girl is flying next!